I am an Aro Publishing
Twenty Word Book

My twenty words are:

Henry	boo
is	he
a	sleeps
cry (cries) (crying)	all
owl	day
has (have)	night
towel	gives
does	animals
not	such
who	fright

ISBN 0-89868-216-9--Library Bound
ISBN 0-89868-217-7-- Soft Bound

FUNNY FARM BOOKS

Henry
the Owl

Story by Wendy Kanno
Pictures by Bob Reese

 ARO PUBLISHING

B

Henry

is

a

crying

owl.

Henry
has
a
crying
towel.

Henry

Owl

does

not

cry

9

Henry
Owl
cries,

"BOO
WHOO
WHOO."

He sleeps all day.

He cries all night.

BOO
WHOO
WHOO

Henry gives animals

such a fright.

Henry is a

crying owl.

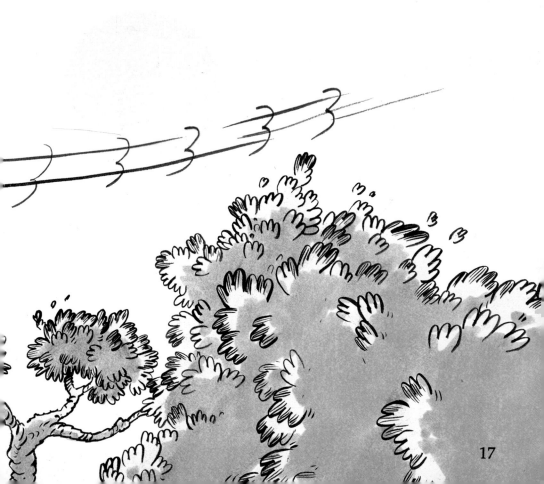

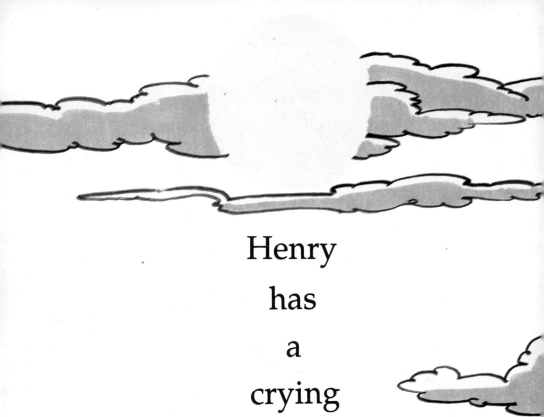

Henry
has
a
crying
towel.

19

Henry
Owl
does
not
cry

Henry
Owl
cries,
"BOO
WHOO
WHOO!"

0/9   11/61   2-6-04